For Georgina
'To see a world in a grain of sand
And a heaven in a wild flower'
from 'Auguries of Innocence' by William Blake
—LH

To my lifelong friend Leena—RV

Little Hare Books
an imprint of
Hardie Grant Egmont
Ground Floor, Building 1, 658 Church Street
Richmond, Victoria 3121, Australia

www.littleharebooks.com

Cataloguing-in-Publication details are available from the National Library of Australia

978 1 760121 48 8 (pbk.)

Designed by Vida & Luke Kelly
Produced by Pica Digital, Singapore
Printed through Asia Pacific Offset
Printed in Shenzhen, Guangdong Province, China

5 4 3 2 1

The illustrations in this book were created 100% digitally.

OUTSIDE

by LIBBY HATHORN
illustrated by RITVA VOUTILA

LITTLE HARE
www.littleharebooks.com

WHAT'S THAT?

It's the fluttery leaves
in the magical breeze
in the summery sun
outside.

WHAT'S THAT?

It's the cat on the stair—
you follow it there,
under fluttery leaves
in the magical breeze
in the summery sun
outside.

WHAT'S THAT?

It's the chime bells up high.
Can you reach them? Just try!
Under fluttery leaves
in the magical breeze
in the summery sun
outside.

WHAT'S THAT?

It's the tickly green grass
and a ball rolling past,
under fluttery leaves
in the magical breeze
in the summery sun
outside.

WHAT'S THAT?

It's the cat with the ball,
the one you let fall
on the tickling grass,
under fluttery leaves
in the magical breeze
in the summery sun
outside.

WHAT'S THAT?

It's a hole in the hedge
where the ball came to rest,
where you and cat hide,
under fluttery leaves
in the magical breeze
in the summery sun
outside.

WHAT'S THAT?

It's our mum come to find
where you and the ball
are hidden so small.

To tickle and hug
then sit on the rug
with the small book that rhymes
and oodles of time,
under fluttery leaves
in the magical breeze
in the summery sun
outside.

WHAT'S THAT?

It's the apple and pear
our mummy put there
that all of us share
outside.

It's a mummy to kiss
and a mummy to cuddle,

then lie on the grass
and see clouds that go past,
hear chime bells that say,
'Why not just stay?'
Under fluttery leaves
in the magical breeze
in the summery sun
outside.

WHAT'S THAT?

It's the smell of our dinner
cooking inside.
Say goodbye to the chimes,
the small book that rhymes,
the big ball that stays
and the cat that still plays,
under fluttery leaves
in the magical breeze
in the summery sun
outside.

Time to step up the step,
one, two, three, four,
and just one step more,
and go right inside.

Wave goodbye!

For tomorrow will shine
with more things to find
under fluttery leaves
in the magical breeze
in the summery sun—
to dance and to twirl
in the beautiful world,
bright and beautiful world—

just outside!

LIBBY HATHORN loves poetry. Reading it, reciting it, teaching it, writing and dreaming about it. Many of her novels and picture books are inspired by poetry, often celebrating nature. Her work has garnered awards and honours both in Australia and internationally, and has been translated into several languages, and adapted to plays, movies and children's operas. In *Outside* she wanted to create a poetic, repetitive text that celebrates a young child's encounter with the outside world and the sense of wonder nature always evokes.

RITVA VOUTILA was born in Finland and has made Australia her home since 1981. She has illustrated numerous children's books including the ever popular *101 Excuses for Not Doing Homework* by Carly Little, the *Lost Island* series by Lisa Thompson, *The Selfish Giant* by Oscar Wilde and *The Stone Lion* by Margaret Wild. For 20 years Ritva has toured all around Australia giving performances and workshops to thousands of school children from Kindergarten to Year 12. She lives in Ballarat with her husband, Richard, and divides her time between illustration and fine art practice. Her website is www.ritvavoutila.com.